For my ma

First published in paperback in Great Britain
by HarperCollins Children's Books in 2009

ISBN-13: 978-0-00-727323-2

10 9 8 7 6 5 4 3 2 1

HarperCollins Children's Books is a division of HarperCollins Publishers Ltd.

Text and illustrations copyright © Emma Chichester Clark 2009
The author/illustrator asserts the moral right to be identified as the author/illustrator of the work.
A CIP catalogue record for this title is available from the British Library.

Visit our website at: www.harpercollins.co.uk

Printed in China

Mummy
and
Me

Emma Chichester Clark

I love doing things
with Mum.

We play
football

and do **gardening**.

We paint
pictures

and read
stories.

I help Mum with cooking

and she says,
"I love doing things **with you, Hum.**"

But one day, she said she had a lot of things
to do, by herself, and I said,

"I'll help you!"

But she said she had to do them by herself.

First, she was on the phone for **ages**.

She said, "**Ssshhh, Hum!** I told you,
I've got **lots of things** to do."

Then she was doing e-mails.
I said, "Are you ready yet?"

But she said, "Not yet, Humber.
Go and find something to do."

But I wanted her to come and play with me.
"Now will you come?" I asked,
and she said, "I will come, Hum,
I promise, but not yet."

"Humber,"
said Mum.
"You **must**
be able to think of
something
to do,
by yourself."

So I tried to think of something.

First,
I jumped
from the
third step
on the stairs.
(The fourth was too high.)

Then I played
football for
a while.

Then I went to
see if I could
find a caterpillar...

and then, I had a
good idea!

I just needed
some things.

Especially,
I needed **mud**…

I put in just the right amount
and **sprinkled** just the
right amount of water.

Then **I mixed**
it all up.

I had to
squelch
it into shape
and put it
on the tray.

Then I needed
flowers
for
decoration.

Next,

I needed some **chairs.**

But then Mum
called me.
"I'm ready now!"
she said.

But I wasn't ready
so I said,
"Just a minute!"

I still needed
to get some things…

I got **cups**

and **cushions**

and the **pies.**

Mum said,
"Are you ready yet?"
And I said,
"Not yet, Mum,
but you must
close your eyes!"

"Keep your eyes closed,"
I said.

"Is it much further?"
asked Mum.

"Nearly there!"
I said.

"Okay, you can open them now!"
I told her.

"Wow, Humber!"

said Mum. "May I come in?"

"Come to tea!"

I said.

"Would you like a cookie?" I asked her,
and she said,
"Mmm! My favourite kind."

And I said, "I love doing things with you.
But I did this all by myself!"
"My clever Hum," said Mum.

Have you read all the stories about
Humber and his sister Plum?

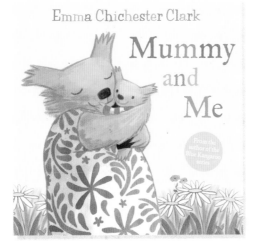

Humber and Plum — Mummy and Me
978-0-00-727323-2 • paperback £5.99

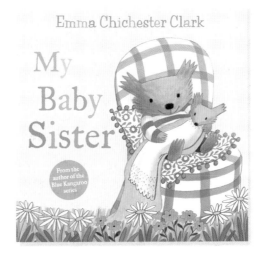

Humber and Plum — My Baby Sister
978-0-00-727324-9 • paperback £5.99

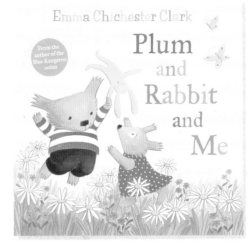

Humber and Plum — Plum and Rabbit and Me
978-0-00-727325-6 • paperback £5.99